*Samuel French Acting Edi*

# Still Alice

*Adapted by*
Christine Mary Dunford

*From the Book by*
Lisa Genova

SAMUELFRENCH.COM SAMUELFRENCH.CO.UK

ISBN 978-0-573-70711-7

www.SamuelFrench.com
www.SamuelFrench.co.uk

**FOR PRODUCTION ENQUIRIES**

United States and Canada
Info@SamuelFrench.com
1-866-598-8449

United Kingdom and Europe
Plays@SamuelFrench.co.uk
020-7255-4302

Each title is subject to availability from Samuel French, depending upon country of performance. Please be aware that *STILL ALICE* may not be licensed by Samuel French in your territory. Professional and amateur producers should contact the nearest Samuel French office or licensing partner to verify availability.

## MUSIC USE NOTE



## IMPORTANT BILLING AND CREDIT REQUIREMENTS

Christine Mary Dunford's stage adaptation of *STILL ALICE,* book by Lisa Genova, was originally developed and produced by the Lookingglass Theatre Company in Chicago, Illinois, where it had its world premiere on April 20, 2013. The production was directed by Christine Mary Dunford*, with scenic design by John Musial*, costume design by Alison Siple*, lighting design by Mike Durst, projection design by Mike Tutaj, sound design by Rick Sims*, and prop design by Maria DeFabo. The associate director/dramaturg was Marti Lyons. The cast was as follows:

**ALICE**.............................................Eva Barr*
**HERSELF**.................................Mariann Mayberry
**JOHN**..........................................Chris Donahue
**THOMAS**.................................Cliff Chamberlain
**LYDIA**.........................................Joanne Dubach
**DR. TAMARA & OTHERS**...........................Tracy Walsh*
**DR. DAVIS & OTHERS** ........................ David L. Kersnar*

* indicates Lookingglass ensemble member or artistic associate

*Still Alice* is a recipient of an Edgerton Foundation New American Plays award.

Christine Mary Dunford received a Joseph Jefferson Nomination for Best New Adaptation in 2013.

*Still Alice*, the book by Lisa Genova, was originally published by Simon & Schuster.

*STILL ALICE* premiered in the United Kingdom as a West Yorkshire Playhouse Production in association with Michael Park for The Infinite Group on February 9, 2018. The production was directed by David Grindley, with set and costume design by Jonathan Fensom, lighting design by Jason Taylor, and sound design by Gregory Clarke. The cast was as follows:

**ALICE**.......................................... Sharon Small
**HERSELF**........................................ Ruth Gemmell
**JOHN**..........................................Dominic Mafham
**THOMAS**........................................ Andrew Rothney
**LYDIA**..........................................Alaïs Lawson
**DR. TAMARA / BETH**.............................. Clara Indrani
**DR. DAVIS / DAN** ...............................Micah Balfour

*STILL ALICE* was the headline production for the Leeds Playhouse (formerly West Yorkshire Playhouse) "Every Third Minute," a festival promoting "theatre, dementia and hope."

The UK tour of *STILL ALICE* ran from September 15 – November 24, 2018 in ten cities. The production was directed by David Grindley, with set and costume design by Jonathan Fensom, lighting design by Jason Taylor, and sound design by Gregory Clarke. The cast was as follows:

**ALICE**.......................................... Sharon Small
**HERSELF**........................................... Eva Pope
**JOHN**..........................................Martin Marquez
**THOMAS**........................................ Mark Armstrong
**LYDIA**...........................................Ruth Ollman
**DR. TAMARA / BETH**...............................Anna Andresen
**DR. DAVIS / DAN** ...............................Micah Balfour

## CHARACTERS

**ALICE** – Fifty years old. Cognitive psychology professor at Harvard University. Driven. Ambitious. Practical. Enjoys being serious, but has a sense of humor. Deeply committed to her work. A respected leader in her field. About to be diagnosed with early-onset Alzheimer's disease. Can hear and talk with Herself.

**HERSELF** – Played by an actress who looks the same age as Alice. Herself and Alice are the same person in two bodies. She is Alice's inner thoughts. However, Herself and Alice can, and often do, have different thoughts in the same moment. She is not Alice's "well" self, or her rational self. She is not omniscient. She progresses through the disease at the same pace as Alice, although she may have moments of lucidity that are different from Alice. She talks directly with Alice (and at others). She appreciates dark humor. Only Alice sees or hears Herself.

**JOHN** – Alice's husband. A biology researcher/professor at Harvard University. Brilliant. Outgoing and friendly. Ambitious. He finds comfort in research, facts, and action. Deeply committed to his research. Begins to be recognized as a leader in his field after Alice is diagnosed.

**THOMAS** – Son of Alice and John. Late twenties. Litigation attorney. A little self-focused. Has always been very close to Alice. Married. Trying to have a child.

**LYDIA** – Daughter of Alice and John. Mid-twenties. An artist/actor. Brilliant, but not interested in traditional formal education. Alice never supported her career choice.

**DR. TAMARA** – Alice's doctor for many years. They are on a first-name basis. (Also plays **BETH.**)

**DR. DAVIS** – Neurologist. Specializes in Alzheimer's disease and related dementias. (Also plays **DAN.**)

## AUTHOR'S NOTE

This is not a play about dying from Alzheimer's disease; it is a play about living with Alzheimer's disease. It is important to resist playing the end of the play from the beginning; to resist making it a play about inevitable loss of memory and death. When considering Alzheimer's disease it is very easy for many of us to fall into the trap of going quickly to a place of sadness or fear. This does not help the play. To avoid this trap, it might be helpful not to consider it a play about Alzheimer's disease at all; but, rather, to consider it a play about living with rapid, uncontrollable change, including memory loss.

It also might be helpful to consider that, while the characters in the play do feel sad for themselves, or for Alice, in (very few) moments, they do not dwell in sadness or self-pity. All of the characters are problem solvers by profession – scientists, attorneys, artists – and each attempts to solve the problem of Alice's illness in their own way. They also live fast-paced lives filled with projects and deadlines; and the pace of the play is generally quite fast, except where noted. Emotion for these characters almost always feels like a surprise. This is true for Alice and Herself as well. Alice and Herself are simply one person represented, through the magic of theatre, by two people. This device provides the audience with a wider window into Alice's mind; or into how Alice makes sense of things that are complex and difficult to understand or accept. Herself can also serve, in very few moments, as a type of narrator to/for the audience. Alice and Herself are always in the same moment together; however, they might be in different places on the stage, in different frames of mind, and/or have different objectives in a moment. For example, while Alice is intent on reprimanding her daughter for not going to college, Herself might be intent on finishing her daughter's uneaten breakfast. Or, while Alice is diligently out running, Herself might be lazily sitting at home reading mail at the kitchen table. Or, when Alice becomes lost in her own neighborhood and overwhelmed by panic, Herself might calm her by directing them both to identify familiar landmarks. Occasionally, one or both of them finds dark humor in their situation. As the play – and the disease – progresses, Alice and Herself live less in the past and the future and more in the present moment. They become grateful for the delicious taste of an ice cream cone; for the sublime beauty of a slant of light streaming into a church; for the joy of talking with someone about a favorite play; or for the comfort of sitting on a lovely beach with a nice person.

Ultimately, *Still Alice* begs questions like: How long are we still ourselves? And, how long do others around us – our family, friends, colleagues – still consider us ourselves when we are changing in ways that are difficult for them to recognize or accept? And, in the end, the play reassures us that Alice and Herself have each other, even after others are out of reach.

The play takes place over two years, from March 2010 to April 2013. Either through projections, through Herself changing a calendar, or through some other device, the audience follows the progression of time through the dates at the top of each scene. Actual dates in the last half of the script may be replaced by phrases such as "a few months later" as long as the original timeline is maintained. Productions have the option to change specific place and institution references in the script (such as "Cape Cod" and "Harvard University") in order to locate the play in a local urban area with a major medical research university. At the top, the set includes specific furniture pieces and props that represent and indicate multiple locations in Alice's life (e.g. home kitchen, school office, etc.). Various clocks onstage may be set to different times. Throughout the play, the stage empties of objects and detail until there is little left except Alice, Herself, and John. The character Herself is onstage whenever Alice is, and can move or remove props and furniture, etc.

## Scene One

*[March 2010]*

*(Early morning.* **ALICE** *is at the kitchen table with her laptop, trying to finish writing a paper to submit for publication.* **HERSELF** *enters and sets the time on a clock as she addresses the audience.)*

**HERSELF.** Even as much as two, three, four, or more, years earlier there were neurons in my head – not far from my ears – that were being strangled to death by plaques and tangles, too quietly for me to hear them. The neurons were unable to warn me before they died. Slowly or quickly, one after another...

**ALICE.** I just read the same sentence three times and still don't understand it.

**HERSELF.** So?

**ALICE.** *(To* **HERSELF. HERSELF** *to audience.)* I wrote it.

**HERSELF.** Take a break.

**ALICE.** Can't. I have to submit this to *Cognitive Psychology* by noon.

**JOHN.** Ali?

**ALICE.** *(Realizes with panic.)* Oh my god. It's 7:30!

**HERSELF.** That's ten minutes fast.

**ALICE.** Why are none of the clocks in this house right?!

**JOHN.** *(Offstage.)* Ali?!

*(***JOHN** *enters, looking around.)*

**ALICE.** Keys?

**JOHN.** Glasses.

*(***ALICE** *picks up his glasses, in open view, on top of the counter.)*

**ALICE.** Glasses. Try pretending you're me while you look.

**JOHN.** Did you get any sleep?

**ALICE.** Some.

**JOHN.** *(Realizes.)* I'm late.

**ALICE.** Go.

*(**JOHN** gets lunch items from fridge, maybe a piece of fruit from the counter. **ALICE** goes back to her computer.)*

**HERSELF.** The microwave says you have tons of time.

**ALICE.** I'm going to take the microwave in.

**JOHN.** No, I told you, I'll fix it.

*(**ALICE** gives **JOHN** a dubious look.)*

Really, I will.

**ALICE.** You don't have time, and it's probably got a computer in it.

*(**JOHN**'s phone rings.)*

**JOHN.** Yeah. I bet you a foot rub I can fix it!

*(**JOHN** picks up the phone. Listens a second...)*

Yes? No, I haven't checked my email yet. What?

*(Listens for a second, then whispers to **ALICE**.)*

We got word about the grant!

*(Collapses physically but not vocally.)*

Really? Well, we knew this could happen.

*(Listens.)*

Yeah. It sucks to be so close, again. Who knows so far?

*(Listens for a second, then serious...)*

Okay. Let me tell everyone else. I'm coming in.

*(**JOHN** slumps.)*

**ALICE.** I'm sorry.

**JOHN.** I thought we had this one, Ali. Three years. Full funding.

**ALICE.** It will happen. I know it will. You know it will. It's just a matter of time.

**JOHN.** I'm running out of time. *(Pause.)* Sorry. *(Pause.)* Sometimes it feels like all I do is write grants. *(Looks at watch.)* Ugh!

*(***ALICE** *and* **HERSELF** *watch* **JOHN** *continue to get ready to leave, admiring him.)*

**ALICE.** Will you be home when I get back?

**JOHN.** *(Putting on a sweater and going to the door.)* I don't know. I have a huge lab day Monday. *(Steps back in to kiss her quickly.)* Give Lydia a hug from me. Try not to fight with her.

**ALICE.** Why would I fight with her? I'm not going to fight with her. I'm only there for a few hours. We won't have time to fight. Be home. I'll make dinner and we can watch –

**JOHN.** I'll try. *(Out the door, but turns back again.)* Wait, where are you going before L.A.?

**ALICE.** I'm going...

*(***ALICE** *does not remember and begins to check her phone.* **HERSELF** *checks her own phone at the same time.)*

**JOHN.** Oh, yeah, Stanford. Have fun.

*(***JOHN** *kisses her again and runs out.)*

**ALICE.** Is he all right?

**HERSELF.** He'll be all right.

## Scene Two

*[March 2010]*

*(***ALICE*** and ***LYDIA*** are in a restaurant in L.A. finishing lunch.* ***HERSELF*** *is sitting at a table next to them, or serving.* ***ALICE*** *checks her phone a few times during the conversation.)*

**LYDIA.** So how's Dad's *Science* paper coming?

**ALICE.** Great. It's done. *(Surprised.)* How did you know he was writing a paper for *Science*?

**HERSELF.** They must have talked recently.

**ALICE.** He didn't mention you'd talked.

**LYDIA.** He called yesterday to tell me about the grant. Pretty awful, huh?

**ALICE.** Yeah. *(Realizing.)* You talked about the *Science* paper yesterday?

**LYDIA.** No. That was last week...or maybe the week before.

**HERSELF.** You haven't talked since Christmas.

**LYDIA.** I should call you more. Or, you should call me. *(Changing the subject.)* Thomas is good?

**ALICE.** Oh, he's wonderful. You haven't seen his new home yet. Five bedrooms, an office for Mattie –

**LYDIA.** That's nice.

**ALICE.** – A TV as big as –

**LYDIA.** How was your meeting yesterday? Did you give a paper?

**ALICE.** Yes. Fine. Fine. *(Checks her phone.)* I have to go in twenty minutes to make my flight. *(Puts phone down.)* I love speaking, you know, all the concatenated moments – teaching, telling a story, provoking debate, the adrenaline of performance.

**LYDIA.** What'd you talk about?

**ALICE.** *(Clearly excited.)* The mental processes that underlie the acquisition and the... *(Can't think of the word.)* ...um...the...oh, goodness, jet lag...the, you know, the putting together in a way...of language. *(Laughs.)* What's the word?

**LYDIA & HERSELF.** Organization?

**ALICE.** Organization! The acquisition and organization of language. *(Checks phone again.)* I want tea.

(**HERSELF** *pours tea for* **ALICE**.)

So, three years in L.A., huh? Wow. So...what do you do all day?

**LYDIA.** Mom...

**ALICE.** Are you in anything? A play?

**LYDIA.** I work at Starbucks during the week, and waitress on Wednesday and Saturday nights.

**ALICE.** That doesn't seem to leave much time for acting.

**LYDIA.** No. I'm not cast in anything right now, but I'm taking workshop classes, and I'm auditioning a lot.

**ALICE.** *(Nods.)* Are you in anything? A play?

**LYDIA.** Mom, I just told you. Why don't you listen to me?

**HERSELF.** You asked the same question twice.

**LYDIA.** I'm taking classes. Meisner technique. I've been auditioning a lot lately.

**ALICE.** *(Has said this many times.)* You're smart, Lydia. You're really smart. It's not too late. You could get into any school. If Thomas can get into –

**LYDIA.** I'm not Thomas, and I don't need college, Mom. I'm fine.

**ALICE.** You can't live like this forever. Are you going to work at Starbucks when you're thirty?

**LYDIA.** Do you know what you're going to be doing in eight years?

**HERSELF.** Yes.

**ALICE.** You could be serving up Venti Lattes with low-fat double steamed something whatever. You should be in college learning something.

**LYDIA.** I am learning something! I'm just not sitting in a Ivy League classroom killing myself trying to get an A in political science.

**ALICE.** Lower your voice.

**LYDIA.** Don't tell me what to do. I'm in an acting class for fifteen hours a week. How many hours a week do your students take, twelve?

**ALICE.** It's not the same thing.

**LYDIA.** Well, Dad thinks it is. He's paying for it.

**HERSELF.** He's what?!

**LYDIA.** You've never even seen me act. At least Dad came out last winter, but you –

**ALICE.** I know. I wish I could have. I was –

**ALICE & LYDIA.** – Swamped.

**ALICE.** *(Pause.)* What will you do if acting doesn't work? How long are you going to sit out here?

**LYDIA.** *(Overlapping with* **ALICE.***)* I'm not *sitting* out here!

**ALICE.** – It's reckless. Without an education –

**LYDIA.** I am getting an education! Mom *(Deep sigh.)* ...Let's go. You're going to miss your flight.

**ALICE.** *(Checking phone.)* No, I'm not. Not yet. I still have ten minutes...eleven.

**LYDIA.** *(Getting up.)* We'll *I'm* going to be late for something.

*(***ALICE** *gets up, leaves money, and they walk away.* **LYDIA** *notices* **ALICE***'s luggage still at the table and stops her.)*

Mom, you forgot your stuff.

## Scene Three

*[March 2010]*

*(***ALICE** *enters her darkened home, pulling luggage. Turns on a light.)*

**ALICE.** John? *(No answer.)* I'm home. John? Fuck.

**HERSELF.** No big deal.

**ALICE.** He said he'd be home.

*(***HERSELF** *makes herself at home.)*

**HERSELF.** He said he'd try. He might have been here and gone back to the lab.

*(***ALICE** *checks answering machine and refrigerator for note.* **THOMAS** *is on the machine.)*

**THOMAS.** Hi, Mom. It's 1:45. And I'm sittin' here eating egg drop soup alone. Without you. Something come up? Call me. Love you.

**HERSELF.** Today's Monday.

**ALICE.** I forgot to cancel lunch with Thomas. *(Back to John.)* John could have called or left a note or *something*.

**HERSELF.** You've done it to him a hundred times. In the middle of work you can't leave. That's what you do. That's what *we* do to each other.

*(***HERSELF** *brings* **ALICE** *her running shoes.)*

**ALICE.** Yeah. You're right. I need a run. *(Realizing.)* Why haven't I been running?!

**HERSELF.** A run will feel good.

*(Through the following,* **ALICE** *runs. We hear her breathing, heavy.)*

I've been thinking about Mom, her hands –

**ALICE.** Her veins –

**HERSELF.** She'd sit there at the table, moving the fork and spoon, placing them, up and then down on the side of her plate –

**HERSELF & ALICE.** – By Dad.

**HERSELF.** As we sat there after dinner, half listening to him talk –

**HERSELF & ALICE.** – On and on –

**HERSELF.** About nothing.

**ALICE.** Mom never exercised.

**HERSELF.** She walked.

**ALICE.** *(Remembering, correcting herself.)* She walked! *(Stops, confused.)* Where am I?

**HERSELF.** Cambridge. Eliot and Brattle.

**ALICE.** *(Naming what she knows.)* Harvard Square's that way, and Kennedy School, but... I don't know... Which way is home?

**HERSELF.** South?

**ALICE.** South.

*(During the following,* **ALICE** *begins to run in one direction, then another, then another. She begins to feel panic and is breathing hard. The wind picks up.)*

**HERSELF.** The Yard. The Old Burial Ground. Maybe...

**ALICE.** It's all familiar. I just can't get my bearings.

**HERSELF.** Left...

**ALICE.** *(Stops.)* Oh, my god. Stop this, please. *(Starts to hyperventilate.)* I want to go home.

**HERSELF.** Langdon!

*(***ALICE** *looks up, sees her front door, and walks in. She is sweating and confused.* **JOHN** *walks in from the kitchen, eating a popsicle. He's unshaven and has been up for two days. He's excited and on the way out.)*

**JOHN.** Hey, I was wondering where you were, just about to leave you a note on the fridge. How'd it go?

**ALICE.** What?

**JOHN.** Stanford.

**ALICE.** Fine.

**JOHN.** And how's Lydia?

**ALICE.** *(Remembering. Angry.)* You're paying for her classes?!

**JOHN.** *(Grabbing a sweater.)* Yes, Ali, we can talk about this later. I don't have time now.

**ALICE.** Make time. John, you're keeping her afloat out there and not telling me?! You're not here when I get home...

**JOHN.** *(Not upset. Gentle, but making a point.)* You weren't here when I got home. How was your run?

**HERSELF.** I got lost.

**ALICE.** Fine.

**JOHN.** Good. *(Excited.)* Listen, I've had an incredible day so far, gorgeous results. I came home to say hi, but I've got to prep for tomorrow.

**ALICE.** How long have you been paying for Lydia's classes?

**JOHN.** I'll talk about this later.

**ALICE.** No. I want to talk now...

**JOHN.** Ali, we agree to disagree about Lydia. It can wait until I get back.

**ALICE.** No, it can't wait.

**JOHN.** Walk over with me, and we can talk on the way.

**ALICE.** I'm not going anywhere. I need to be home.

**JOHN.** *(Puzzled.)* You need to be home? Look, the sooner I go, the sooner I'll be back. Take a nap. You look tired. I'll be home as soon as I can.

*(**JOHN** leaves. **ALICE** sinks to the floor. She watches her hands shake in her lap.)*

**ALICE.** Menopause?

*(**HERSELF** is on the computer at the kitchen table googling "menopause" and "symptoms.")*

**HERSELF.** "Menopause." "Symptoms." It's a long list. Hot flashes, night sweats, insomnia, fatigue, anxiety, dizziness, irregular heartbeat, depression, irritability...

(**HERSELF** *looks over at* **ALICE** *like "you've got that one all right."* **ALICE** *laughs a little at* **HERSELF**.*)*

**HERSELF.** I'm just sayin'. *(Continues reading.)* Mental confusion, memory lapses, disorientation.

**ALICE.** Check. Check. Check.

**HERSELF.** *(Still reading from the internet.)* Millions of women cope with it every day.

**ALICE.** Nothing abnormal.

*(To* **HERSELF**.*)* I'll make an appointment with Tamara for a check-up. Maybe go on estrogen replacement. God. *(Laughs.)* I'm getting old, I guess.

## Scene Four

*[June 2010]*

*(**ALICE** puts on a dress and fixes her hair. **HERSELF** is "mirroring" **ALICE** some of the time.)*

**ALICE.** I don't look like I imagine I do anymore. My neck is wrinkled.

**HERSELF.** And you care because...?

**ALICE.** It's going to keep getting more wrinkled.

**HERSELF.** I think there are wrinkly neck exercises you can do.

**ALICE.** I got my period this morning.

**HERSELF.** According to the all-knowing internet, menstruation at the beginning of menopause is often irregular, and doesn't disappear all at once.

**ALICE.** Really?

**HERSELF.** Really. Ready?

**ALICE.** Ready.

**HERSELF.** Let's have a little birthday fun...

*(**THOMAS** enters in a business suit, with a cake. It is a fiftieth birthday party for Alice. An 8x10 photo of Lydia is at the table.)*

**THOMAS.** Happy birthday, Mom! Oh my god, fifty! You don't look a day over...oh, I don't know...forty-nine and three-quarters.

**HERSELF.** *(Laughing.)* He tries...

**ALICE.** Thank you, Tommy. I see you finally found your razor.

**THOMAS.** *(Laughing.)* Yeah.

**ALICE.** What did you bring?

**THOMAS.** Yellow cake, chocolate frosting. My favorite.

**ALICE.** Ah. Too bad there's not enough for you.

*(**JOHN** enters with champagne and pours through the following.)*

**THOMAS.** Yeah. Hi Dad.

**ALICE.** Where's Mattie?

**THOMAS.** She's stuck at work. She'll text about running over to campus later this week.

**JOHN.** How is she?

**THOMAS.** Fine. The same. Worried. About a case. About getting pregnant. About how she'll work if she actually *does* get pregnant. I don't know how you did it, Mom, with the two of us in grad school.

**HERSELF.** Waddling, pushing, pumping, cleaning up poop.

**THOMAS.** Mom?

**ALICE.** She'll figure it out. *(Gives him a big hug or something.)* How are *you*?

**THOMAS.** Good, really good. I'm taking a case to John Adams.

**ALICE.** Tom! That's fantastic!

**JOHN.** Our boy's arguing a case in the oldest court in the land!

**ALICE.** That's great!

**THOMAS.** I know, right?! It's good. I'm good.

**ALICE.** So, when is it?

**THOMAS.** I don't know. It hasn't been scheduled yet. I'll let you know.

*(**JOHN** raises his glass to toast **THOMAS**.)*

No, no, no. Let's not toast to how awesome I am. It's Mom's birthday.

*(**THOMAS** gestures to the picture of Lydia.)*

God, when was the last time Lydia came to one of our birthday parties? Five years at least. My twenty-first!

**JOHN.** No, it couldn't be...

**HERSELF.** *(Realizing.)* He's jealous of Lydia.

**THOMAS.** I'm pretty sure it was.

**HERSELF.** Because she's smarter than he is.

**JOHN.** She was here for my fiftieth three years ago. We went on an architecture cruise and you got sick, remember?

**THOMAS.** I can't believe she's still out there. I mean, what's she doing?

**JOHN.** She's working.

**THOMAS.** On a play?

**ALICE.** She's got two jobs. She's waiting tables and she's working at Starbucks.

**HERSELF.** She's a barista.

**ALICE.** She's a barista.

**THOMAS.** She serves coffee.

**JOHN.** She's living the dream in the big city.

**ALICE.** She's taking classes.

**JOHN.** She's taking classes. *(Raising a glass of champagne.)* Happy birthday to my beautiful and brilliant wife.

**THOMAS.** To your next fifty years!

## Scene Five

*[July 2010]*

*(Dr. Tamara's office.* **ALICE** *is sitting in a chair next to an examining table.* **HERSELF** *is on the table, fidgeting with something she found in the office. We are catching* **ALICE** *and* **DR. TAMARA** *mid-conversation.)*

**ALICE.** *(Upbeat. No big deal.)* I've been forgetting little things, and I think I might be pre-menopausal. I stopped getting my period about six months ago, but it came back last month, so I thought maybe I'm *not* in menopause, and then, well, I thought I should talk to you.

**DR. TAMARA.** What kinds of things are you forgetting?

**ALICE.** Names, words in conversation.

**HERSELF.** My phone.

*(***DR. TAMARA** *types in her computer.)*

**ALICE.** I also became disoriented on a run. I didn't know where I was for a couple of minutes before it all just came back to me. Strange.

*(***DR. TAMARA** *stops writing and turns to* **ALICE.** **HERSELF** *notices and stops what she was doing.)*

**DR. TAMARA.** Did you have any tightness in your chest? Numbness or tingling?

**ALICE.** No.

*(***DR. TAMARA***'s questions come fairly fast and direct, like she is going through a checklist.)*

**DR. TAMARA.** Headache or dizziness?

**ALICE.** No.

**DR. TAMARA.** Heart palpitations?

**ALICE.** My heart was pounding, but that was after I became confused.

**HERSELF.** More like an adrenaline response to being scared.

**DR. TAMARA.** Okay. How are you sleeping?

**ALICE & HERSELF.** Fine.

**ALICE.** About five or six hours a night.

**DR. TAMARA.** This is usual for you, right?

**ALICE.** Yes.

**DR. TAMARA.** Do you have trouble falling asleep, or staying asleep?

**ALICE.** No.

**DR. TAMARA.** Any unusual stress? At home? At work?

*(**ALICE** shakes her head "no.")*

**HERSELF.** I like stress.

**DR. TAMARA.** Heartburn, weight change, or bleeding in your urine or bowel movements?

**HERSELF.** *(Grossed out.)* What? Really?!

**ALICE.** No.

**DR. TAMARA.** Could you be depressed?

**ALICE.** I was depressed for a year after my mother and sister were killed in a car accident. This is not that.

**HERSELF.** This is not a job for Prozac.

**DR. TAMARA.** Are you taking medications for anything?

**ALICE.** Just a multivitamin.

**DR. TAMARA.** Drinking?

**ALICE.** You know, socially. A glass of wine with dinner sometimes. No street drugs.

*("No street drugs" was **ALICE**'s attempt at a joke. **DR. TAMARA** does not laugh. She taps her pen as she reads her notes.)*

**HERSELF.** So...

**ALICE.** What do you think? Am I in menopause?

**DR. TAMARA.** We'll run an FSH, but I don't think your memory problems are due to menopause.

*(Pause.)*

**HERSELF.** *(Frustrated that she's not answering quickly.)* Why not?

**DR. TAMARA.** The symptoms of memory disturbances and disorientation listed for menopause are secondary to poor sleep hygiene. It's possible that you are not sleeping as well as you think you are.

**ALICE.** If I'm sleeping fine?

**HERSELF.** What are you thinking?

**DR. TAMARA.** I'm concerned about the disorientation. I want to do some tests. I'll send you for blood work, you had a mammogram, bone density because it's time, and an MRI.

**HERSELF.** *(Surprised and scared.)* A brain tumor?!

**ALICE.** What are you looking for with an MRI?

**DR. TAMARA.** It's always good to rule things out. Get the MRI and see me after. Okay?

**ALICE.** Thank you.

**HERSELF.** Lovely. Dr. Tamara didn't answer the question.

## Scene Six

*[October 2010]*

*(It is dark.* **JOHN** *is in the kitchen.* **ALICE** *and* **HERSELF** *enter the house.* **ALICE** *is in her robe and slippers, carrying her laptop briefcase.)*

**JOHN.** Ali?

**ALICE.** What?

**JOHN.** Where were you?

**HERSELF.** What do you mean?

**JOHN.** I got up and you weren't here. Where were you?

**ALICE.** At school. My office is quiet today. No one was there.

**JOHN.** It's six a.m. *(Pause.)* You went to school in your robe, honey?

**HERSELF.** And your bunny slippers?

**ALICE.** Fuck.

### Scene Seven

*[November 2010]*

*(In Dr. Tamara's office. We are catching* **ALICE** *and* **DR. TAMARA** *mid-conversation.)*

**DR. TAMARA.** Your blood work came back normal, and your MRI is clean. We can do one of two things. We can wait, see how things go, see how you're doing in three months. Or, you can –

**HERSELF & ALICE.** I want to see a neurologist.

**DR. TAMARA.** I'll give you a referral. You'll need to bring John to your first appointment.

**HERSELF.** Say what?

**ALICE.** Why? John's busy.

**DR. TAMARA.** You're having a problem with your memory. He might be the most reliable source for what's going on.

**HERSELF.** Shit.

**ALICE.** Okay...

## Scene Eight

*[December 2010]*

*(***ALICE, HERSELF,** *and* **JOHN** *are at a department office Christmas party. Alice's graduate student* **DAN** *is there, and his wife* **BETH.** *Christmas music is in the background.** **ALICE** *and* **JOHN** *are drinking wine and are in a festive mood.* **HERSELF** *is having a good time, too. Maybe she is serving with a tray and eating some herself.)*

**JOHN.** The dean brought fourteen different kinds of cakes, pies and cookies. A personal best, I believe.

**ALICE.** I hear it took ten pounds of butter, and three days. I'm particularly fond of the peanut butter pie with chocolate crust.

**HERSELF.** I had it in the cafeteria when I was a girl.

**ALICE.** *(Grimaces and laughs at* **HERSELF.***)* Funny. Peanut butter pie makes me think of the grade school cafeteria...

**HERSELF.** Where you felt safe.

*(***DAN** *walks in with* **BETH.***)*

**DAN.** Professors, I'd like you to meet my wife, Beth.

**ALICE.** Dan, she does exist! So nice to meet you, Beth. Congratulations!

*(Shaking hands with* **BETH.***)*

**BETH.** Thank you. Nice to meet you, too. Dan has told me so much about you.

**ALICE.** Dan, congratulations! You know my husband, John. John, you remember one of my star students, Dan.

**JOHN.** *(Shakes hands.)* Congratulations! Let's find you both a drink. So, how do you like married life so far?

---

*A license to produce *Still Alice* does not include a performance license for any third-party or copyrighted music. Licensees should create an original composition or use music in the public domain. For further information, please see Music Use Note on page 3.

*(The three of them walk away from* **ALICE** *to get drinks.* **HERSELF** *and* **ALICE**, *now alone, sit at a piano.)*

**HERSELF.** I wish I could play piano.

**ALICE.** Annie and I took lessons.

**HERSELF.** But now I can only remember the right hand of "Baby Elephant Walk."

**ALICE.** Annie played the left. I miss her.

**HERSELF.** And Mom.

**ALICE.** I miss my mom. *(To* **HERSELF**.*)* I'm sad tonight.

**HERSELF.** Holiday parties can do that.

*(***BETH, DAN,** *and* **JOHN** *come back with drinks.)*

**ALICE.** Hello. *(Smiles at* **BETH**.*)* I'm Alice Howland. I don't believe we've met.

**BETH.** *(Looks nervously at* **JOHN**.*)* I'm Beth.

**ALICE.** Are you our new postdoc?

**BETH.** No, I'm Dan's wife.

**ALICE.** Oh! Wonderful. So nice to finally meet you! Dan, congratulations! Well done!

*(***DAN** *and* **BETH** *exchange glances. They look to* **JOHN**, *who takes* **ALICE**'*s wine glass and smiles at* **DAN** *and* **BETH**.*)*

**JOHN.** Wow. Someone's having fun.

**ALICE.** What? *(To* **HERSELF**.*)* What?

**HERSELF.** I don't know. Give me my wine!

**ALICE.** *(To* **JOHN**, *as she takes her wine glass back.)* What?

## Scene Nine

*[December 25, 2010]*

*(It's early Christmas morning.* **ALICE** *and* **HERSELF** *are going through photo albums on the couch, sipping tea.)*

**HERSELF.** Thomas, one, in Wales when I gave that talk in London. He had just started walking and had a big bump on his head. Lydia in her itchy, powder-blue costume at her first dance recital. *(Laughs and points.)* Look at her hands, oh my gosh! Lydia in braces. Thomas at prom. He was sick with love for that girl on his baseball team.

**ALICE.** I don't need labels. I remember it all.

*(***JOHN** *enters.)*

**JOHN.** I'm going to the lab for an hour.

**ALICE.** Today?!

**JOHN.** Just for a few minutes, then I'll pick Lydia up at the airport. What time is Thomas coming?

**ALICE.** *(Looking at the photo album.)* Around noon. Mattie's coming later. She's going by her mom's for a while. The roast is in. I'll start...soon.

**JOHN.** Okay.

*(***JOHN** *exits.)*

**ALICE.** I'm going to write down random words, and see if I can remember them every half hour.

*(***HERSELF** *hands* **ALICE** *a pad of paper.)*

**HERSELF.** Okay.

*(***HERSELF** *goes into the kitchen.)*

**ALICE.** Tambourine, serpent.

**HERSELF.** Stethoscope.

**ALICE.** Millennium.

**HERSELF.** Hedgehog.

**ALICE**. Trellis.
**HERSELF**. Vanish.
**ALICE**. *(To* **HERSELF**.*)* Remember those.

## Scene Ten

*[December 25, 2010]*

*(Around 1:30 p.m.* **JOHN** *and* **THOMAS** *are in the living room playing Scrabble.* **LYDIA** *and* **ALICE** *are in the kitchen.* **LYDIA** *is stirring hot mulled cider.* **ALICE** *is getting out ingredients to make white-chocolate bread pudding, a tradition. She keeps checking the oven, puzzled.)*

**LYDIA.** *(Excited.)* Everything has a purpose, you know. We worked on the Greeks for a month. More! You know, Antigone, Electra, Oedipus the King? I used to think that they were so emotional, but they're not at all. Emotion just happens when needs aren't met. Like, Antigone has to bury her brother, but she can't because it's against the law, but she has to or he will never go on to the afterlife. It's about being pulled in different directions, you know? It translates to everything else... Shakespeare...even plays today. And acting-wise, thinking about it like this makes it so much easier to act, except it's not easy...at all.

**ALICE.** *(Listening to* **LYDIA.***)* Wow.

**THOMAS.** *(Shouting from the other room.)* Mom, where's the wine opener?

**LYDIA.** Oh my god, Mom, they were using theatre to figure out things like the difference between God's law, civil law, and the rights of people, you know, citizens. They were working out big questions for the first time.

**ALICE.** Right?!

**HERSELF.** Something's wrong with the roast. Tambourine, serpent, stethoscope, millennium...

**THOMAS.** *(Shouting from the other room.)* Mom?!

**LYDIA.** There are no small gestures in the Greeks. No petty personal issues. Nothing is petty. We drove to the ocean and shouted into the wind and the surf...to the gods. To confront powers greater than ourselves.

**HERSELF.** Millennium. Shit! What's after millennium?

**ALICE.** Hedgehog.

**LYDIA.** What?

**HERSELF.** Hedgehog! Hedgehog!

**ALICE.** What's wrong with the roast? It's not roasting.

**LYDIA.** What?

**HERSELF.** Is the oven on? The oven's not on.

**ALICE.** Oh, my *god*! I forgot to turn the oven on. Dinner's going to be late.

**LYDIA.** We eat too early anyway.

**THOMAS.** *(Overlapping* **LYDIA**, *shouting.)* Dad just got a triple word score with the "x"...

**HERSELF.** Very late.

**THOMAS.** ...And I need a drink. Mom? Where's the wine opener.

**ALICE.** *(Shouting back.)* Look around...or ask your father. He's right there!

**LYDIA.** Emotion comes when you can't get what you need most to live.

**ALICE.** Lydia, please, this is fascinating, but I can't hear it right now.

**JOHN.** *(Shouting from the other room.)* Ali, I can't find it!

**LYDIA.** *(Visibly hurt.)* I'll help them look.

*(**LYDIA** exits to play Scrabble with the others. **ALICE** notices her hands shaking and starts to look at them. **HERSELF** starts to make the bread pudding.)*

**HERSELF.** Make the bread pudding. Calm. Like Mom. Okay? Okay. Vanilla extract, heavy cream, milk, sugar, white chocolate, loaf of challah, a dozen eggs.

**ALICE.** A dozen?

**HERSELF.** Yes.

**ALICE.** Is it seven, eight, nine?

**HERSELF.** A dozen!

**ALICE.** *(Realizing that something has changed, perhaps forever.)* Oh my god, I've made this every year for thirty years. *(Looks around like she is seeing things for the first time.)* What pan do I use? Do I use all the cream or only some of it? Sugar? How much sugar? How many eggs?

**HERSELF.** I hate these fucking eggs!

*(**ALICE** starts silently throwing the eggs, slowly and purposely, into the kitchen sink. She starts to cry.)*

*(Quietly.)* Emotion from unmet need.

**ALICE.** Shut up.

*(**ALICE** throws eggs until they are all gone. **LYDIA** is standing in the doorway, watching.)*

**LYDIA.** Mom, what are you doing?

**ALICE.** The eggs were past the expiration date. There's no pudding this year.

**LYDIA.** We have to have pudding.

**ALICE.** Well, there are no more eggs, and I'm tired of standing in this not-hot kitchen.

*(**ALICE** is covered with flour and eggs. **JOHN** and **THOMAS** enter the kitchen.)*

**LYDIA.** Mom?

**JOHN.** What's going on?

**HERSELF.** Tell them.

**THOMAS.** Mom?

**HERSELF.** Just tell them.

**ALICE.** Kids, I'm losing my mind. My memory.

**THOMAS.** What?

**JOHN.** *(She's overstating things.)* You're not losing your mind, Ali.

*(To kids.)* Don't worry. She's fine.

*(To **ALICE**.)* You're going to see the doctor. You're going to find out –

**THOMAS.** Doctor? What's wrong?

**JOHN.** Nothing's wrong. She...we made an appointment with a neurologist to do a workup. He's not going to find anything.

**THOMAS.** What are they looking for?!

**JOHN.** Nothing. *(Correcting himself.)* We don't know. It's probably nothing. She's stressed and she's –

**ALICE.** It's not stress.

**THOMAS.** Jesus, Mom, if something's wrong why didn't you tell me?

**HERSELF.** I'm only just realizing myself.

**THOMAS.** What is it? What are you –

**LYDIA.** Mom's been forgetting things. Simple things that she should know.

**THOMAS.** What?! That's ridiculous. I haven't noticed anything.

**LYDIA.** For a while now. *(Explaining.)* She called me three times to tell me she was coming to Stanford.

**THOMAS.** Oh my god, Lydia, that's crazy. So she called you a couple times –

**LYDIA.** Don't call me crazy! We had repeat conversations. She's talking to herself. She forgot to turn the oven on.

**THOMAS.** The oven! What the hell?! Mom?

**JOHN.** She's probably menopausal. Hormones changing. It's powerful. She could be a little depressed.

**ALICE.** Please, John, even Lydia sees it. Think about it. Remember, I went to the office in my pajamas?

**LYDIA.** "Even Lydia sees it."

**THOMAS.** *(Translating.)* You're never here.

**LYDIA.** That's the point. And even I see it.

*(To* **JOHN.***)* Is she forgetting things she's not aware of?

**HERSELF.** I'm in the room.

**THOMAS.** *(Desperate for it to be true.)* Mom, please, you're not forgetting anything important.

**LYDIA.** Pull your head out, Tom.

**THOMAS.** Shut up, Lydia!

**JOHN**. *(Remembering.)* Dan's wife, Beth, at the Christmas party. *(Realizing.)* You weren't drunk.

**ALICE**. No.

*(***JOHN*** and ***THOMAS*** just stand there.* ***ALICE*** *sinks into a chair.)*

**HERSELF**. I'm going to throw up.

**LYDIA**. I'll make the pudding, Mom. You relax.

*(***LYDIA*** puts her coat on and begins to exit.)*

**THOMAS**. Where are you going?

**LYDIA**. To find a store that's open. *(Turns back.)* Mom, how many eggs do I need?

## Scene Eleven

*[February 2011]*

*(***DR. DAVIS*** sits in a chair across from ***JOHN***. ***DR. DAVIS*** has a clipboard and takes notes occasionally through the following.)*

**DR. DAVIS**. Please, have a seat, Alice. I've just had a few minutes here with John. He's finishing some paperwork. It's good to see you again. I'm going to ask you a few questions.

**JOHN**. Then we can talk about treatment options.

**DR. DAVIS**. Yes.

**ALICE**. *(Referring to the paperwork* **JOHN** *is completing.)* What is that?

**DR. DAVIS**. It's an "Activities of Daily Living" questionnaire. He fills it out every time you both come in, and we look for patterns. *(Smiling at* **ALICE**.*)* How are you?

**ALICE**. *(It's true.)* I'm good.

**HERSELF**. *(Observing* **JOHN**.*)* He's spinning his wedding ring.

*(***ALICE*** looks and notices too.)*

**ALICE**. And wiggling my chair with his foot.

**JOHN**. What?

**ALICE**. Nothing.

**HERSELF**. Never did that before.

**DR. DAVIS**. How about your memory? Have there been changes? Any concerns?

**ALICE**. I'm having a hard time keeping track of my schedule. *(Deep sigh.)* And I hate talking on the phone.

**DR. DAVIS**. How about disorientation? Any more getting lost or feeling confused?

**ALICE**. *(Hopeful about this.)* No.

**HERSELF**. *(Remembering.)* Well...

**ALICE**. *(Remembering! Happy she remembers.)* Right. Sometimes I get confused about what time of day it is. *(A little amused.)* Once I went to the office in the middle of the night.

**DR. DAVIS.** This kind of confusion is quite common and wandering may happen again. You might want to attach a bell to the front door...

**JOHN.** ...A bell? Like in a shop?!

**DR. DAVIS.** *(Calm.)* ...Or something that would wake you up. *(Back to* **ALICE.***)* There's a program called Medic Alert Safe Return. You register with them and get an I.D. bracelet with a code on it.

**ALICE.** I have John programmed into my phone.

**DR. DAVIS.** That's good. *(A real question.)* But what happens if the battery goes dead or John's phone is off, and you get lost?

**HERSELF.** What about –

**ALICE & HERSELF.** – A piece of paper! –

**ALICE.** – In my bag that has my name, John's, our address and phone number?

**DR. DAVIS.** That could work, but what if you forget your bag?

**JOHN.** With the bracelet you wouldn't have to think about anything, Ali. *(To the* **DOCTOR.***)* We'll get one.

**HERSELF.** We will?

**DR. DAVIS.** How are you doing with your medications? Taking all your doses?

**ALICE.** Yes.

**DR. DAVIS.** Any side effects. Nausea? Dizziness? Trouble sleeping?

**ALICE.** No.

**DR. DAVIS.** Are you getting exercise?

**ALICE.** I'm running about five miles most days.

*(Laughing with* **HERSELF** *at the irony.)*

I have to or I lose my mind!

**DR. DAVIS.** *(Laughs with* **ALICE.***)* John, do you run?

*(***HERSELF** *laughs abruptly at the thought.)*

**JOHN.** *(Confused about why they are laughing.)* I walk to work and home. I swim sometimes.

**DR. DAVIS.** I think it'd be good for you to start running with Alice. She enjoys it, and research suggests that exercise can slow the accumulation of amyloid-beta and cognitive decline.

**HERSELF.** He hates running.

**JOHN.** *(Not excited.)* I'll start running with her.

**ALICE.** *(Excited.)* Thomas could run with me.

**JOHN.** I'll run with you.

**DR. DAVIS.** Have you told anyone at Harvard yet?

**ALICE.** No.

**DR. DAVIS.** Were you able to teach your classes this quarter?

**ALICE.** *(Sad.)* Umm... Well –

**HERSELF.** *(Realizing. Not upset. Fascinated and kind of amused in an odd sort of way.)* Someday my brain will be in the hand of a medical student. Bloodless. Formaline-perfused, Silly-Putty colored.

**JOHN.** Alice?

**ALICE.** Sort of.

**HERSELF.** The instructor will point to various sulci and gyri, indicating the locations of the somatosensory cortex –

**ALICE.** *(To* **DAVIS.***)* I'm travelling less. *(Realizing.)* I used to travel a lot.

*(To* **JOHN**, *with an idea.)* John, we could go to the cottage!

**JOHN.** *(To* **ALICE**, *doubtful.)* We could go for a few weeks. *(Explaining to* **DR. DAVIS.***)* We have a place by the sea on Cape Cod.

**DR. DAVIS.** That sounds wonderful.

**HERSELF.** Soon I will forget the smell of the grass by the sea –

**DR. DAVIS.** Alice, I think you should come up with a plan for the fall that involves telling people at Harvard.

**ALICE.** Yes.

**HERSELF.** The names of my children, the sound of their voices –

**DR. DAVIS.** Maybe come up with a way to transition from your job.

**HERSELF.** *(Looking at* **JOHN.***)* John's name. His face. His hands –

**DR. DAVIS.** There are some legal things you should plan. Advance directives like power of attorney and a living will.

**ALICE.** Yes.

**DR. DAVIS.** Have you thought about whether or not you'd like to donate your brain to research?

**ALICE.** Yes.

**JOHN.** *(Overlapping* **ALICE***, a little shocked at the doctor's casualness.)* We can talk about that later.

**HERSELF.** Of course.

**DR. DAVIS.** Okay. John, can I have that paper? Thank you.

**HERSELF.** They will cut my brain into thin, coronal slices –

**DR. DAVIS.** How would you say Alice is doing?

**JOHN.** Fine.

**HERSELF.** – Like a deli ham –

**JOHN.** She lets her phone go to voicemail most of the time.

**HERSELF.** – They will adhere it to glass slides so students will be able to see the empty spaces where I once resided.

**JOHN.** But she's glued to her calendar – like a compulsion. Checks it every minute. It's a little difficult to watch.

**HERSELF.** *(Gently. Realizing.)* I'm becoming difficult to look at.

**DR. DAVIS.** Anything else that Alice hasn't mentioned?

**HERSELF.** *(Realizing.)* When he can look, I'm like an experiment.

**JOHN.** No.

**HERSELF.** One of his lab rats.

**DR. DAVIS.** How's her mood and personality, any changes?

**JOHN.** No, she's the same. Maybe a little defensive.

**HERSELF.** *(Defensive.)* I am?!

**JOHN.** And quieter, she doesn't see friends, or initiate conversation much.

**ALICE.** I don't?

**HERSELF.** Wow...

**DR. DAVIS.** And how are you?

**JOHN.** Me? *(Surprised at the question.)* I'm fine.

**DR. DAVIS.** We have a caregiver's support group. I'd like you to make an appointment...

**JOHN.** An appointment for me?

**DR. DAVIS.** Yes.

**JOHN.** I don't need one. I'm fine.

**DR. DAVIS.** It can become difficult. If you want to talk with someone later...

*(**JOHN** waves him away.)*

Okay.

*(**DR. DAVIS** turns to **ALICE**.)*

And now, Alice, let's start our questions.

**ALICE.** The same ones as last time?

**DR. DAVIS.** Yes. What day of the week is it?

**ALICE.** Monday.

**DR. DAVIS.** When were you born?

**ALICE.** June 10, 1960.

**DR. DAVIS.** Who is the Vice President of the United States?

**ALICE.** *(Just a touch of pride that she knows.)* Joe Biden.

**DR. DAVIS.** Okay, now, I'm going to tell you a name and address, and you repeat it back to me. I'm going to ask you to repeat it again later, okay? John Black, 32 West Street, Belmont.

**ALICE.** John Black, 32 West Street, Belmont.

**HERSELF.** *(Trying to lock it into her memory.)* John Black, 32 West Street, Belmont. John never wears black –

**DR. DAVIS.** Okay. Can you count to twenty forwards and then backwards?

**ALICE & HERSELF.** Yes.

**HERSELF.** *(While* **ALICE** *starts to count.)* ...Lydia lives out west. The horse race Belmont Stakes... Thirty-two years ago I was eighteen...

**ALICE.** *(Pause, smile.)* Zero, one, two, three, four, five, six, seven, eight, nine, ten, eleven, twelve, thirteen, fourteen, fifteen, sixteen, seventeen, eighteen, nineteen, twenty...

**ALICE & HERSELF.** ...Twenty, nineteen, eighteen, seventeen, sixteen, fifteen, fourteen, thirteen, twelve, eleven, ten, nine, eight, seven, six, five, four, three, two, one.

**HERSELF.** Zero.

**ALICE.** Zero!

**DR. DAVIS.** Good. Now, what is this thing on my watch called?

**ALICE.** *(Having a little fun now.)* A clasp.

**DR. DAVIS.** On this paper, draw a clock that shows the time forty-five minutes past three.

> *(***ALICE** *draws a big circle and then writes the numbers one through twelve, but puts all of the numbers inside the right side of the circle so that one is at the top and twelve is at the bottom where the six should be. The left side of the clock face is blank.)*

**HERSELF.** All the numbers are on one side. I don't think that's right.

**ALICE.** Oops, I made the circle too big.

> *(***ALICE** *scribbles the picture of the clock out and writes "3:45.")*

**JOHN.** Not digital.

**DR. DAVIS.** I'm looking for an analog clock.

**HERSELF.** *(To* **JOHN.***)* Whose side are you on?

**ALICE.** Draw me a clock face, and I'll show you 3:45.

> *(***DR. DAVIS** *turns the first paper over and draws a clock with numbers on it.)*

**DR. DAVIS.** *(To* **JOHN.***)* Parietal lobes are affected pretty early on and that's where we keep our internal representations of extra-personal space –

**HERSELF.** Defend me!

**DR. DAVIS.** – This is why I want you to go running with her.

*(**ALICE** takes the paper and draws hands on it.)*

**ALICE.** There's 3:45.

**DR. DAVIS.** Okay. Now, I'd like you to tell me the name and address I asked you to remember earlier.

**ALICE.** John Black, something West, Belmont.

**DR. DAVIS.** Okay. Was it 32, 34, 36, or 38?

**ALICE.** 38.

*(**DR. DAVIS** starts writing something lengthy on his clipboard. **JOHN** has been unconsciously wiggling **ALICE**'s chair with his foot.)*

John, please stop shaking my chair.

**DR. DAVIS.** Now we can start talking about clinical trials.

*(**JOHN** sits up in his seat. This has been what he's been waiting for.)*

**HERSELF.** Just tell him it's progressive and fatal, and let's go.

**DR. DAVIS.** There are several ongoing studies here in Boston. One I like best, Amylix, appears to bind celluloid amyloid-beta and prevent its aggression. The phase two study was encouraging.

**JOHN.** I assume it's placebo-controlled?

**DR. DAVIS.** Yes.

**JOHN.** What do you think about the secretase inhibitors?

*(**ALICE** looks at **HERSELF** for explanation.)*

**DR. DAVIS.** Right now the secretase inhibitors are too toxic for clinical use.

**JOHN.** What about Bapinuzemab?

**DR. DAVIS.** Yes. There's a lot of attention on that one, but –

**JOHN.** How do you feel about flurbiprofin?

**DR. DAVIS.** We don't have the data yet.

**JOHN.** Elan's monoclonal antibody?

**DR. DAVIS.** That trial has been discontinued.

**JOHN.** IVIg therapy?

**DR. DAVIS.** We don't know the proper dosing. I'm not against it. Untargeted. Crude. Expensive and not reimbursable by insurance.

**JOHN.** But it's worth it if it works.

**DR. DAVIS.** Yes. I wouldn't expect its effects to be anything more than modest.

**JOHN.** I'll take modest. Alice would be guaranteed not to be in a placebo group. How long would she be in trial?

**DR. DAVIS.** It's a fifteen-month study.

**ALICE.** What's your wife's name?

**DR. DAVIS.** Mary.

**ALICE.** What would you want Mary to do if she had this?

**DR. DAVIS.** I'd want her to enroll in the Amylix trial.

**JOHN.** *(To both of them.)* I think we should do the IVIg along with flurbiprofen. Alice?

**ALICE.** I want to do the Amylix trial.

**JOHN.** I think you should trust me on this, Ali.

**ALICE.** I've done the reading, too.

*(To* **DR. DAVIS.***)* I want to do the trial.

**DR. DAVIS.** Okay.

**HERSELF.** *(Narrating the moment like she's narrating the action in a film.)* Dr. Davis leaves the room. My husband spins his wedding ring. I think...

*(***HERSELF** *pulls out two matching Medical Alert bracelets and gives one to* **ALICE***. They put them on together.)*

*(To* **ALICE.***)* Stay here.

### Scene Twelve

*[May 2011]*

*(It's the first warm spring day. Through the following,* **ALICE** *and* **HERSELF** *share an ice cream cone and walk around campus.)*

**HERSELF.** Double-scoop Peanut Butter Cup in a sugar cone.

**ALICE.** No more frozen yogurt. Hell, I'm on –

**ALICE & HERSELF.** Lipitor.

**ALICE.** I'd forgotten how great ice cream is! It's so nice out. Let's just walk. Maybe the chapel is open.

**HERSELF.** Chapel?!

**ALICE.** It's pretty. Do you think the doors might be open?

**HERSELF.** Let's find out.

**ALICE.** I wish I had cancer. I'd have something I could fight. People could rally behind me and do a 5K. Cook vegan dinner for us on Wednesday nights. If I died from it, I'd be able to look people in the eye –

**HERSELF & ALICE.** – Know who they were –

**ALICE.** – And say good-bye before I left. *(Pause.)* The kids could have it... *(Realizing.)* And Tom and Mattie are trying to have a baby. Oh god.

**HERSELF.** Someday they too might not be able to talk, walk, feed themselves, recognize their children. They might curl up in a fetal position, forget to swallow and get pneumonia. Their children might –

**ALICE.** You're ruining my ice cream.

**HERSELF.** I'm just sayin'.

**ALICE.** *(Looks around. Light from stained glass fills the space.)* Isn't this beautiful? See how the light looks like butterflies.

**HERSELF.** Remember when you caught a butterfly and you told Mom you were going to keep it in a jar forever.

**ALICE.** She said I should let it go because butterflies only live for a few days, and I cried.

**HERSELF.** She said not to be sad for butterflies, remember?

**ALICE.** Their lives are short.

**HERSELF.** But they are not tragic. *(A statement.)* They have beautiful, short lives.

**ALICE.** I have a beautiful life.

**HERSELF.** *(To* **ALICE.***)* What do I want to do before I die?

**ALICE.** Wow! Um... Hold Tom and Mattie's baby. Smell its feet. See Lydia actually act in something. Spend a year with John hanging out at the cottage.
*(To* **HERSELF.***)* We could do that, you know.

**HERSELF.** If he wanted.

**ALICE.** He's got sabbatical in two years. *(Sigh.)* I want to read every book I can before I can no longer read. Novels. I never read enough novels.

**HERSELF.** At least one trashy novel.

**ALICE.** And history. I want to learn to paint with watercolors. I suppose I might have to learn to draw first, though. Do you think?

**HERSELF.** *(Observing.)* No Harvard? No research? No teaching? No concatenated moments?

**ALICE.** *(Realizing. Laughing.)* Oh my goodness, wow, I guess not. *(Finishes ice cream.)* I want more days like this and ice cream cones. When I can no longer appreciate the pleasure of an ice cream cone, I think it's time to go, don't you?

*(***ALICE** *pulls out her phone and starts to type.* **HERSELF** *reads what she writes.)*

**HERSELF.** Alice, answer the following questions: What month is it?

**ALICE.** May.

**HERSELF.** Where do you live? 34 Langdon Street, Cambridge, MA 02138. Where is your office?

**ALICE.** William James Hall, room 1002. When is Thomas' birthday? November 7, 1984.

**HERSELF.** How many children do you have?

**ALICE.** Two.

**HERSELF.** If you have trouble answering any of these, go to the file named "butterfly" –

**ALICE.** Nice.

**HERSELF.** – On your computer and follow the instructions.

**ALICE.** I'll set a reminder for 3:00 every day, with no end date.

## Scene Thirteen

*[June 2011]*

*(**ALICE** sits in Dr. Tamara's office with her phone in her lap.)*

**DR. TAMARA.** It's taking you over an hour to get to sleep?

**ALICE.** Yes, and then I wake up a couple hours after that and go through the whole thing all over again.

**HERSELF.** *(Coaching.)* Look more tired.

*(**ALICE** sighs and slumps a little, taking **HERSELF**'s direction.)*

**DR. TAMARA.** What medications are you taking?

**ALICE.** Aricept, Namenda, Lipitor, vitamins C and E, and Aspirin.

**DR. TAMARA.** Insomnia can be a side effect of Aricept.

**ALICE.** Right. Well, I'm not going off Aricept.

**DR. TAMARA.** What do you do when you can't get to sleep?

**ALICE.** Mostly I lie there and worry –

**HERSELF.** *(Finishing thought, matter-of-fact.)* – That I might wake up and not know where I am or who I am.

**DR. TAMARA.** I could prescribe you an SSRI.

**ALICE.** I'm not depressed.

**DR. TAMARA.** We could try you on Restoril. You'll sleep for about six hours...

**ALICE.** I'd like something stronger.

*(**DR. TAMARA** stops and looks at **ALICE**. **ALICE** and **HERSELF** look steadily at **DR. TAMARA**.)*

**DR. TAMARA.** I think I'd like you to come back with John to talk about prescribing something –

**ALICE.** This doesn't concern my husband. *(Assuring **DR. TAMARA**.)* I'm not depressed, and I'm not desperate. I'm aware of what I'm asking for, Tamara.

**HERSELF.** I'll see another doctor if I have to.

**DR. TAMARA**. All right, Alice.

*(***DR. TAMARA*** starts typing a prescription.)*

**ALICE**. Thank you.

## Scene Fourteen

*[November 2011]*

*(**JOHN** is painting the trim on the house. **HERSELF** is painting too.)*

**ALICE.** John?

*(**ALICE** is walking through the house when her phone alarm goes off. She stops and answers the following questions quickly, like she has done it many times.)*

November. 34 Langdon Street, Cambridge. William James Hall. November 7. Two. John?

**HERSELF.** *(Shouting.)* He's outside painting the house! Can you believe it?!

**ALICE.** I've been looking for you.

**JOHN.** I was out here. I didn't hear you.

**ALICE.** Are you going to that conference today?

**JOHN.** Monday. Tomorrow.

**ALICE.** That's after Lydia gets here, right?

**JOHN.** Yes. She'll be here this afternoon. Are you ready to run?

**ALICE.** Yes. It's a little cold. Let me grab a fleece.

*(**JOHN** and **HERSELF** keep painting. **ALICE** goes in, gets a fleece, notices a book, picks it up, goes to the kitchen, turns a kettle on for water, sits down, and starts to read. **JOHN** comes in.)*

**JOHN.** What are you doing? Aren't we going for a run?

**ALICE.** Oh yes, I'd like to go for a run. This book is making me crazy.

**JOHN.** So, let's go running.

**ALICE.** Are you going to that conference today?

**JOHN.** Monday.

**ALICE.** What's today?

**JOHN.** Sunday.

**ALICE.** Oh, and when does Thomas get here? Before you leave?

**JOHN.** No, Ali. Lydia's coming, not Thomas. She gets here this afternoon. You should put this in your phone.

**ALICE.** Okay.

**JOHN.** Ready to go?

**ALICE.** Yes. Wait, let me pee first.

**JOHN.** All right, I'll be out by the garage.

*(**JOHN** goes to the garage. **ALICE** puts the book down and is ready to move but does not remember what she was going to do. **HERSELF** enters the kitchen, goes to put the kettle on, and sees that it's already on. Through the following, she gets things out to make tea. **ALICE** walks into the kitchen.)*

**ALICE.** What did I come in here for? A fleece!

**HERSELF.** You already have one.

**ALICE.** Oh, I don't remember. To hell with it, I'm going running.

*(**ALICE** walks toward the door, then realizes...)*

I have to pee!

*(**ALICE** runs down the hall and stops.)*

Where's the bathroom?!

**HERSELF.** That's the utility closet.

**ALICE.** I know. Where's the bathroom?

**HERSELF.** Where it's always been.

*(**ALICE** runs around the house as **HERSELF** narrates where she is.)*

Back door. Living room. Dining room. Kitchen.

**ALICE.** *(To **HERSELF**, angry.)* How can I be lost in my own house?!

*(**ALICE** is completely panicked. She starts to shake and cry. She also pees her pants, standing in the middle of the kitchen. **JOHN** enters.)*

**JOHN.** Ali?

**ALICE.** Don't look at me!

**JOHN.** Ali, don't cry. It's okay.

**ALICE.** I can't find the bathroom. I wet my pants.

**JOHN.** It's okay, you're right here.

**ALICE.** It's not okay.

**HERSELF.** I'm lost.

**JOHN.** Ali, it's okay. You're with me.

## Scene Fifteen

*[November 2011]*

*(The whistle from the tea kettle goes off.* **HERSELF** *turns off the burner and starts to make tea for herself,* **LYDIA**, *and* **ALICE**, *who are sitting at the kitchen table. Play scripts are open in front of them.)*

**ALICE.** *(Telling the story to* **LYDIA**, *who has never heard it before directly from her mother.)* My mother, and sister, Anne, died when I was a freshman in college. My first week. My second day in the dorm the TA came to my room. He knocked before he came in. The door was open. "Alice? There has been an accident." My father was drunk, and drove them into a tree. He lived. I don't talk to him.

**HERSELF.** *(To* **ALICE**.*)* He died last year. Of liver failure.

**ALICE.** *(To* **HERSELF**.*)* Right. *(To* **LYDIA**.*)* I took the quarter off.

**LYDIA.** Mom, that must have been really hard.

*(***HERSELF** *puts tea, mini-bagels, butter, and crème cheese in front of them, then cleans up the counter.* **ALICE** *begins to serve herself.)*

**ALICE.** I'm glad you left L.A. and came to do a play here.

**LYDIA.** I'm just here auditioning, Mom. But if I get in the play I'll be back here next summer. That would be fun, wouldn't it? We could read more plays!

**ALICE.** I like reading plays with you. It smells different.

**LYDIA.** *(Surprised.)* What does?

**ALICE.** Los Angeles. They're shorter than books, plays, and they're broken up into scenes. I can handle scenes. Can you please get the um...spreads like butter but tastes different...um...the...

**LYDIA.** Crème cheese. *(Passes the crème cheese.)* I hope I get cast. Everyone else at the audition had BFAs or MFAs and is a lot older. But I felt okay. Really. They seemed to take me seriously. *(Joking a little.)* I must have learned something in L.A.

**ALICE.** What about going to school for a degree in theatre?

**LYDIA.** Mom, please, stop. Don't you understand what I was just saying? I don't need a degree.

**ALICE.** I heard every word that you said, and I understood it. I'm not doubting that you could have a career as an actor, but what if you decide that you want to teach –

**LYDIA.** *You* teach, not me –

**ALICE.** I know, but do you think you might want to have a family someday? *(Pause. Starts to doodle something.)* Life only gets busier. You're going to want some options. Maybe talk with some of the people you audition with about what it's like to be relying only on acting in your thirties and forties... Maybe. Just consider it. Okay?

**LYDIA.** Okay.

**HERSELF.** Oh my god. That's the closest she's come to agreeing with you since...maybe never!

**LYDIA.** What does it feel like?

**ALICE.** What?

**LYDIA.** Alzheimer's disease. Can you feel that you have it right now?

**ALICE.** Well, I know I'm not confused or repeating myself right now, but just a minute ago I couldn't find "crème cheese." It's only a matter of time before it happens again. Even when I feel completely normal I know I'm not.

**HERSELF.** I don't trust myself.

**LYDIA.** So you know when it's happening.

**ALICE.** Most of the time. *(Smiles.)* I think.

**LYDIA.** Like, what was happening when you couldn't think of the word for crème cheese?

**ALICE.** I know what I'm looking for but my brain can't get to it. It's like...like if you decided that you wanted that cup of tea, only your hand won't pick it up.

**LYDIA.** That sounds like torture.
**HERSELF.** It is.
**LYDIA.** I'm so sorry you have this.
**HERSELF.** I hope you don't get it.
**ALICE.** Thank you.

## Scene Sixteen

*[March 2012]*

*(***ALICE*** is stretching in running shoes and a t-shirt that says, "This is what awesome looks like." Unfolded laundry and papers are around the house. It's a mess. There are Stick'em notes everywhere for Alice. Repeat of the action at the opening of the play. Early morning, but it's raining outside.* **ALICE** *watches* **JOHN***, who is now dressed in suit and tie, making a lot of noise, walking fast through the house, looking for his glasses.)*

**JOHN.** *(Frustrated.)* Why are none of the clocks in this house right?

**ALICE.** The microwave says you have tons of time.

*(***ALICE***'s phone goes off. She is distracted by* **JOHN** *and doesn't notice the phone.)*

**HERSELF.** It's your questions.

**JOHN.** Do we have to have Stick'ems everywhere?!

**ALICE.** Keys?

**JOHN.** No. *(Phone goes off again.)* Do you want to get your phone?

**ALICE.** March. Langdon, Cambridge. William James Hall. November. Two.

**JOHN.** What?

**ALICE.** What are you looking for?

**JOHN.** Nothing.

**ALICE.** Let me help. I can help you.

**JOHN.** It's okay, Ali.

**ALICE.** I'm good at looking. Glasses?

*(***ALICE*** walks to the kitchen counter and picks up John's glasses, in open view. Hands them to* **JOHN***.)*

**JOHN.** *(Grabs them and runs to the door.)* Thanks.

**ALICE.** I thought we were going for a run.

**JOHN.** *(Getting his work things together.)* No, Ali, remember. I have a really important meeting. I will be home this afternoon...or...this evening, and we can go running. Do *not* go out without me, okay? Thomas is coming. Promise.

**ALICE.** Yes.

*(**JOHN** kisses **ALICE** on the head and exits. A shop doorbell tinkles. **ALICE** sits on the floor where she is, pulls her knees to her chest, and starts to rock back and forth. **ALICE** takes out her phone and dials **JOHN**.)*

John? *(Happy, as if she just had the idea and is calling him.)* Let's go for a run. *(Listens. Disappointed.)* Okay.

*(**ALICE** hangs up, but dials again with a solution.)*

John? Turn around and come home. *(Listens, getting sad.)* I don't care if it's raining. Go to your meeting later. *(Listens. Impatient.)* No, now! *(Listens. Angry.)* Fuck you!

*(**ALICE** hangs up the phone and sits with her knees to her chest, watching the door. **HERSELF** takes the phone from **ALICE** and throws it in the freezer. **ALICE** notices a big, open hole where there was once a rug by the front door.)*

Has that hole always been there? How do people get to the door?

**HERSELF.** What hole?

**ALICE.** Do they walk around it?

**HERSELF.** Oh my god. I'm not sure. Something's wrong, I think.

*(**HERSELF** goes to examine the hole.)*

**ALICE.** Don't go near it!

*(**HERSELF** backs off. **ALICE** continues to watch the door. She starts to hum, then moan. **HERSELF** hears this and goes to sit next to **ALICE**.)*

**HERSELF.** What's wrong?

**ALICE.** *(Matter-of-fact.)* There's a hole in the floor; I'm trapped in my house; and I didn't recognize my face in the mirror this morning.

**HERSELF.** *(Upset she's not getting more credit.)* I recognized you! I told you it was you!

**ALICE.** It took you five seconds. An eternity. It shouldn't take that long. What happens when you don't remember at all?

**HERSELF.** I may not remember who you are, but I'll still be here, with you. I'm not going anywhere.

**ALICE.** I'm scared.

**HERSELF.** Me too. *(Pause. Gets an idea...)* If I forget you, I will just get to know you again.

**ALICE.** Over and over again?

**HERSELF.** Yes. I like you.

*(A shop doorbell tinkles.* **THOMAS** *enters from the back, dressed in a suit, hair wet from the rain. He is carrying a Chinese take-out bag and an armful of towels.)*

**ALICE.** John?

*(The hole disappears and the rug reappears.)*

**THOMAS.** No, it's me, Mom. Sorry I'm so late. You must be starving. I brought Chinese. Mom, this mountain of towels was blocking the back door. You can't do that. *(Realizing.)* How long have you been sitting there?

**ALICE.** Um... Since John left.

**THOMAS.** This morning?! Mom...?

**ALICE.** I've been listening to a buzzer going off. I thought it was the phone, but it wasn't.

**HERSELF.** I know because I answered the phone, but no one was there. Maybe because it was the TV remote.

**ALICE.** *(Referring to the mystery of the buzzer.)* It was the microwave. I just figured it out! What smells?

**THOMAS.** Why didn't you call me?

**ALICE.** My phone isn't working. What stinks?

**THOMAS.** I don't know. Chinese maybe? You like Chinese. There's a fortune cookie for you. What happened to your phone?

**HERSELF.** I put it in the freezer by accident, and it froze to death.

**ALICE.** *(Suddenly very angry.)* Whatever it is, get it out of here, I can't stand it. I hate it when you do that!

**THOMAS.** What?

**ALICE.** Bring something that stinks! You always do that. *(Realizes that she's still in running clothes, and cold.)* Should I get changed?

**THOMAS.** Sure, change if you want to.

*(**THOMAS** puts the food in the refrigerator and starts to fold towels and clean the house. **ALICE** starts to help him.)*

**ALICE.** Where's John?

**THOMAS.** He's in Maryland meeting with the folks at the National Institute of Health.

**HERSELF.** Maryland?

**ALICE.** No. He's going running with me.

**THOMAS.** I'm sure he'll be home soon.

**ALICE.** Where's Anne?

**THOMAS.** Anne? Who?

**HERSELF.** My sister.

**ALICE.** Anne.

**THOMAS.** *(Stops cleaning.)* Your sister?

**ALICE.** Yes, my sister.

**THOMAS.** Mom, Anne's dead. She died in a car accident with your mother. Your father...

*(**ALICE** freezes and starts to shake. She collapses to her knees. She begins to cry. **HERSELF** goes to her, holds her in her arms and rocks her gently.)*

Mom?

**HERSELF**. *(Singing.)* It's okay. It's all right. It's okay. It's all right. It's okay. It's all right.

**THOMAS**. No, Mom, no, this happened a long time ago, remember?

*(A shop bell rings and* **JOHN** *enters, still in a suit, happy and energized. He also has a package with a bow wrapped around it.)*

**JOHN**. What's wrong?

**THOMAS**. She was asking for Anne. She thinks they just died.

**JOHN**. Oh my god.

**ALICE**. *(Accusing* **JOHN**. *Very confused and angry.)* You've known about this. You've been keeping it from me! You've been keeping things from me!

**JOHN**. No, Alice. No. I'm not keeping anything from you. You're confused. Anne and your mother died a long time ago. When you were in college. It was a long time ago. A long time ago, Ali. You're okay. It's okay now.

*(Silence.* **HERSELF** *hums to* **ALICE**, *who takes a deep breath, gets her bearings, and collects herself. She sits up.* **JOHN** *puts his things away.)*

**ALICE**. What were you doing in Maryland?

**JOHN**. What? Ali, honey, nothing, a meeting.

**HERSELF**. He's lying.

**ALICE**. You told me you were going to work, not another state. *(Realizing.)* Did you fly?!

**THOMAS**. Dad, tell her...

**JOHN**. Not now...

**THOMAS**. Yes, now. Tell her. She knows something is happening. She's not stupid.

**JOHN**. *(Shocked at this thought.)* Of course she's not stupid. I never said that. I never thought that. I just want to wait until –

**THOMAS**. Tell her.

*(**JOHN** sits by **ALICE** on the floor and puts down the package that he was carrying. **HERSELF** opens it through the following. It is watercolor paints and paper. From this moment through to the end of the play, **HERSELF** finds moments to paint [butterflies] while she participates, more or less, in scene.)*

**JOHN.** Ali, honey, I might be up for a job. A great job at the NIH. Nothing's certain yet. It wouldn't be until fall *next* year, and there'd be a lot to figure out. But if I got it I'd have full funding. And a lab, Ali. I might be able to take two graduate students with me.

**ALICE.** John, that's wonderful!

**THOMAS.** I gotta go. Mattie's going to kill me. I don't think she's eaten. There's Chinese in the fridge, but she doesn't like the smell.

*(To **ALICE**.)* I'll see you, Mom.

*(To **JOHN**.)* I think she needs a new phone.

*(To **ALICE**.)* Love you.

*(**THOMAS** exits. The back door shop bell tinkles.)*

**ALICE.** A lab? John, that's great!

**JOHN.** Nothing's set. I won't know for certain until early next year.

**HERSELF.** He's moving to Maryland.

**ALICE.** *(Realizing.)* You're moving?!

**JOHN.** No, Ali, we *might* be moving. Maybe. But you'd love D.C. It's beautiful. *(He's excited.)* We could find a little home where we can see the Potomac –

**ALICE.** *(Completely clear-thinking. Calm.)* I'm very happy for you, John.

**HERSELF.** But it's not the best timing, is it?

*(**ALICE** gets up and starts putting things away or cleaning.)*

**ALICE.** If they want you next year, they'll want you the year after.

**JOHN.** It's not like that, Ali. There won't be a year after for this one. It would be wonderful –

**ALICE.** We're going to take sabbatical next year, and go to the cottage. Read novels on the beach –

**JOHN.** I never said I was going to take sabbatical. We talked about it, but we never agreed.

**ALICE.** *(Getting upset.)* You never said "no."

**JOHN.** I never said "yes." Honey, you'll love D.C.

**ALICE.** I don't want to move to D.C. I need to say this now, John, while I still can. I don't want to go.

**JOHN.** Think back to what it was like to work. Remember? Remember waking up in the middle of the night because you were too excited to sleep? Remember sitting, arguing about some tiny point that was so important? Ali, if I get this job, I need to take it. Things always seemed to come easy for you, Ali. It's my turn now. I'm getting older, honey, I have to do this. A chance like this won't come again. You know how it works. Ali, if this happens, please be happy for me. I want you to be happy for me.

**HERSELF.** We never spent enough time together.

**ALICE.** You left me alone for too long.

**JOHN.** What? Ali, I'm sorry. I meant to be home earlier, but the director asked me to dinner and I knew Thomas was coming, so I took a later flight. We can go running tomorrow morning, I promise...

**ALICE.** No, not today, our whole lives.

**JOHN.** *(Very serious. He's been thinking about this.)* That's not true, Ali. *(Slowly.)* We've lived together for twenty-five years. We work –

**HERSELF.** Worked.

**JOHN.** – At the same place. We've spent our lives together.

**ALICE.** In the beginning we did, but it changed.

**HERSELF.** We've lived next to each other.

**JOHN.** No, Ali. We've liked our lives. I like our lives. You've liked our lives. I think we've had a good balance. We've each had our work – our passion – the kids, and each other. You loved your work, almost more than anything. You had fun. Haven't you liked our life?

**ALICE.** We're talking in the past tense.

**JOHN.** Ali...

**HERSELF.** He needs to get up. His knees are killing him.

**ALICE.** Yes, John. I've liked our lives.

**JOHN.** *(Kisses her head.)* I love you. I'm going to change...

*(***JOHN** *exits.* **ALICE** *sits and watches* **HERSELF** *paint. She's hasn't changed, and is still cold.* **ALICE** *shivers.)*

## Scene Seventeen

*[June 2012]*

*(**HERSELF** helps **ALICE** change. **ALICE**, **LYDIA**, and **JOHN** are waiting for Thomas and getting ready to go to dinner before an evening performance of Lydia's play.)*

**LYDIA.** Mom, are you ready?

**HERSELF.** Lydia's play!

**ALICE.** Yes, almost.

**JOHN.** Hey, star of the show! Are you ready to go?

**LYDIA.** Yes. Where's Thomas?

**JOHN.** Late. Always late.

*(**THOMAS** enters.)*

**THOMAS.** Mom, Dad, Lydia! Sorry I'm so late. We just got great news. Mattie's pregnant!

**JOHN.** *(Hugging **THOMAS**.)* How far along, do you think?

**THOMAS.** About seven weeks, we think.

**JOHN.** *(To **ALICE**.)* Did you hear that? You're going to be a grandmother!

*(Everyone but **ALICE** starts to talk at once, giving congratulations, asking questions. **THOMAS** notices **ALICE** looking at her hands.)*

**THOMAS.** Mom, how are you feeling?

**ALICE.** *(Just fine.)* Mostly good.

**JOHN.** She's been doing great. I'll get the car.

*(**JOHN** exits.)*

**HERSELF.** Why?

**THOMAS.** You seem quiet.

**LYDIA.** There are too many people talking at once too quickly.

**ALICE.** I'm very happy for you. *(Pulling her phone from her pocket.)* Lydia, what time is your performance?

**LYDIA.** 7:30. I'm leaving for the theater now. You're going with everyone to dinner and then you're going to meet me there.

**THOMAS.** Are you nervous?

**LYDIA.** A little. Critics will be there. You'll be there. But once I get going, I'll be fine.

**ALICE.** Lydia, what time is your play?

**THOMAS.** Mom, you just asked that. Don't worry about it.

**ALICE.** I did? Okay. What time?

(**THOMAS** *kindly pushes her phone aside.)*

**THOMAS.** It doesn't matter. You'll just stick with us.

**LYDIA.** It's at 7:30. Tom, you're not helping.

**THOMAS.** No, you're not helping. Why should she worry about remembering something she doesn't have to remember?

**LYDIA.** She won't worry about it if she puts it in her phone. Just let her do it.

**THOMAS.** Well, really, she shouldn't be relying on her phone anyway. She should be exercising her memory whenever she can.

**LYDIA.** So, which is it? Should she be memorizing my show time or totally relying on us?

**THOMAS.** Lydia, you can't just drop in whenever it's convenient and start acting like you know something. Look, Mom, what time is Lydia's show?

**ALICE.** I don't know; that's why I asked her.

**THOMAS.** She told you the answer twice, Mom. Try to remember what she said.

**ALICE.** I was going to enter it in my phone but you interrupted me.

**THOMAS.** I'm not asking you to look it up. Mom, just think for a second.

**HERSELF.** Stop quizzing me.

**ALICE.** *(To* **LYDIA.***)* Lydia, what time is your show?

**LYDIA.** 7:30.

**ALICE.** *(To* **TOM.***)* Lydia's show is at 7:30.

**LYDIA.** I gotta go.

*(**LYDIA** hugs **ALICE** and then exits.)*

## Scene Eighteen

*[June 2012]*

*(**ALICE**, **JOHN**, and **TOM** are waiting to meet **LYDIA** in front of house after her play. There are sounds of people talking and laughing. The play was a big hit. **ALICE** is beaming, enjoying a bunch of flowers she is holding for Lydia, not paying attention at first to **JOHN** and **TOM**, who enter in mid-conversation.)*

**THOMAS.** I don't want Mom stuck in one of those places.

**JOHN.** *(Calm.)* She's not going to be *stuck* anywhere. And it's not "one of those places." It's great. She would be doing things, with people, instead of sitting at home alone all day.

**HERSELF.** I think they're talking about you.

**ALICE.** Smell this. What is this flower?

**THOMAS.** What about having someone come in?

**JOHN.** I don't want to talk about it here, Tom. I'm exploring options, that's all.

**ALICE.** *(To **JOHN** and **THOMAS**.)* We should go to more plays!

*(**LYDIA** enters. Everyone hugs and kisses through the following. **ALICE** holds on to flowers she was supposed to give to **LYDIA**.)*

**JOHN.** You were wonderful!

**ALICE.** You were wonderful, really, incredible!

**LYDIA.** *(Beaming.)* Thank you. Isn't it such a great play?

**THOMAS.** You didn't seem nervous at all.

**HERSELF.** *(Joining in.)* Everyone is hugging and kissing!

**ALICE.** Will we get to see you in anything else this season?

*(Everyone stops and looks at **ALICE**.)*

**THOMAS.** What?

**ALICE.** *(To **JOHN**.)* She was beautiful in the play, wasn't she?

**THOMAS.** Mom?

**HERSELF.** Something's wrong.

**ALICE.** Well, I hope we get to see you again. You're really quite good.

**JOHN.** Ali, this is Lydia, our daughter.

## Scene Nineteen

*[July 2012]*

*(**ALICE** is leaning over **HERSELF** at a laptop, giving her directions.)*

**ALICE.** Just type it in!

**HERSELF.** That's. What. I'm. Doing. Stop bossing me!

**ALICE.** I'm not bossing. "S" "u" "p" –

**HERSELF.** I know how to spell "support"! There's only stuff here for caregivers. "For caregivers: visiting the nursing facility, medications, stress relief, dealing with patient aggression, delusions, night wandering..." Eek!

**ALICE.** What about something for people with the *actual* disease?!

**HERSELF.** I don't know! I don't see anything. Call that guy.

**ALICE.** What guy?

**HERSELF.** The memory doctor guy. Ask him.

**ALICE.** I did. He says there're no groups, nothing.

**HERSELF.** Why?!

**ALICE.** I don't know! That's why I'm trying to look it up! What's that? *(Points to screen.)*

**HERSELF.** A file.

**ALICE.** I know it's a file. What file? It's important.

**HERSELF.** How do you know?

**ALICE.** I remember.

**HERSELF.** *(Clicks on file.)* "Butterfly." *(Reading.)* Dear Alice... *(Realizing.)* You wrote this to yourself!

**ALICE.** Okay. Keep reading!

**HERSELF.** Dear Alice, you wrote this letter to yourself *(Looks to **ALICE** like "I told you so.")* when you were of sound mind. Answer the following questions: What month is it? Where do you live? Where is your office? When is Thomas' birthday? How many children do you have? You have Alzheimer's disease. If you cannot answer these questions, then you are no longer of sound mind, and can no longer trust your own judgment. But you can trust mine, your former self. You have lived an extraordinary and worthwhile life. You have been blessed with a great career, a loving husband, and two happy children. I love you, and I am proud of you, and how you lived. Now, go to the dresser in the bedroom. Open the top-left drawer. In the back is a bottle of pills. Swallow all of them at the same time with water. Then, close your eyes and go to sleep. Go now, before you forget. And do not tell anyone what you are doing. Trust me. Alice Howland.

**ALICE.** I don't remember writing it.

**HERSELF.** Do you know the answer to any of the questions?

**ALICE.** No. Oh, I have two children.

**HERSELF.** That was in the letter.

(**ALICE** *takes a deep breath.*)

**ALICE.** Okay. Let's go.

(**ALICE** *and* **HERSELF** *go to the bedroom, take everything out of the drawer.*)

Tissues, pen, pen, pen, pencil, penny... Lots of "p"s. What's this called?

(**ALICE** *holds a small bottle of lotion up.*)

**HERSELF.** "Lotion," floss, ew! A Stick'em with writing on it...

(**JOHN** *enters with a glass of water and pills in his hand.*)

**JOHN.** Alice?

(**ALICE** *and* **HERSELF** *pause like kids caught with their hands in a cookie jar.*)

**ALICE & HERSELF.** What?

**JOHN.** Dr. Davis called. He invited you to give a speech at a big conference. I told him I didn't know and we would talk about it... What are you doing?

**ALICE.** Looking for something. I'd like to give a talk.

**JOHN.** I don't know, Alice. What would you talk about?

**ALICE**. Me. What it's like. Do you know there aren't any groups for people? Only for caregivers. I'm going to start one. Last time I was waiting for you and Dr. Davis I started talking with this nice man. We realized in the same moment that neither of us could remember why we were there and we laughed so hard. It was the first time I felt normal in forever. I'm going to call Dr. Davis and get some names. I could invite them over for coffee. You could make your poppy seed cake –

**JOHN**. Whoa, Alice, slow down. Listen, if you did the conference you'd have to travel, you'd have to remember a whole speech. What if you're having a difficult day? You don't need that kind of stress –

**ALICE**. You would come with me, right?

**JOHN**. Right.

**ALICE**. You'd help me write it, right?

**JOHN**. *(Doubtful.)* Yeah.

**ALICE**. Then it'd be fine.

**JOHN**. I wouldn't be up there with you, Ali. You might not be able to read a whole –

**ALICE**. I know. *(Thinking.)* I won't read it. I'll write the main points down and, what's the word?

**HERSELF**. Make it up... Impro–

**ALICE**. Improvise! It will be fun. *(Pause. Serious.)* Please, John. *(Playful.)* We can watch bad movies all night in the motel.

**JOHN**. Hotel. I don't know, Ali. Let's think about it. I have to run to the post office. I'll only be gone a few minutes.

**ALICE**. Okay.

**JOHN**. Don't go out, okay? Oh. Here. It's time. You need to take these.

*(**JOHN** hands **ALICE** the glass of water and the pills, then quickly exits.)*

**ALICE**. My pills! I was looking for these! Thank you.

*(**ALICE** and **HERSELF** both take the pills.)*

I'm supposed to go to sleep after the pills, right?

**HERSELF.** Right.

*(**ALICE** and **HERSELF** both lay down. Pause.)*

**ALICE.** What if I'm not tired?

**HERSELF.** Shhh!

*(Pause. **ALICE** sits up.)*

**ALICE.** Do you think I laid down long enough?

**HERSELF.** Probably.

*(**ALICE** stands up and starts to exit as **HERSELF** sits there a moment.)*

*(Worried.)* Wait!

*(**ALICE** stops and looks at **HERSELF**.)*

**ALICE.** *(Concerned.)* What?

**HERSELF.** I don't know. I feel like I'm forgetting something really important.

*(They look around and at each other a moment.)*

**ALICE.** *(Still concerned.)* If it's important, someone will remind you.

*(**HERSELF** stands, dropping the contents of the drawer onto the floor. **ALICE** and **HERSELF** exit. **JOHN** enters, finding the mess they left and begins to clean up. He finds the bottle of pills and looks after **ALICE**.)*

**JOHN.** Oh, Ali...

*(**JOHN** breaks down and starts to cry. After a moment, he begins to collect himself and puts the pills in his pocket.)*

## Scene Twenty

*[November 2012]*

*(***ALICE*** is giving the keynote address at the annual Alzheimer's Association Conference. It is a huge honor. Her family sits in the front row, along with* **DR. DAVIS. HERSELF** *sits in the audience.* **JOHN** *starts standing next to* **ALICE. ALICE** *is very lucid throughout her speech.)*

**JOHN.** I'll be right here if you need me. I can –

**ALICE.** I'll be fine, John. I'm feeling fine today.

**HERSELF.** I don't think people give speeches with their husband standing next to them.

**ALICE.** Really. It's okay. I'll be okay. You can sit down.

**JOHN.** Okay.

*(***JOHN*** doesn't move.)*

**HERSELF.** Go get 'em!

*(***ALICE*** clears her throat and begins.)*

**ALICE.** Good afternoon, My name is Dr. Alice Howland. I'm not a, um *(Pause.)* medical doctor. I was a professor at Harvard University for twenty-five years. I taught courses in *(Checks notes.)* cognitive psychology. I did research in *(Checks notes.)* linguistics, and gave talks all over the world. This is my husband, John. He's standing up here because he's worried for me. And he's wearing his lucky experiment t-shirt because he thinks it will bring me good luck. But he doesn't need to stand up here with me. I'm having a good day and will be fine. *(To* **JOHN.***)* You can sit down now.

*(***JOHN*** sits in the front.)*

I'm honored to have this opportunity to talk with you, to tell you what it's like to live with dementia, because I have it and I know. I have prepared a talk, but I may forget parts of it.

**HERSELF.** They didn't get your joke. Say it again.

**ALICE.** That was a joke. "I may forget parts of it." *(Smiles at own joke.)* If I do forget I will check my notes. *(Holds up paper.)* I have young-onset Alzheimer's disease. Soon, although I'll still know what it's like, I won't be able to describe it to you. And soon after that, I'll no longer even know I have dementia. So I have to say this now. What's it like? Well, some days I feel normal. I know who you are and who I am and I carry on with simple tasks like going for a run or doing laundry. I can find the words I want to say, and I don't fall down because I misjudged the distance to the curb. Other days, it feels like I'm living in a mixed-up Dr. Seuss world where simple things like faces or the dial on a washing machine look unfamiliar. I see the girl at the coffee shop make a strange face and I know that I have just done something to make her see me differently. It can be puzzling, frustrating and lonely. Sometimes frightening. To have no control. Change is frightening and my world is changing all the time. However I am not incompetent. I still have opinions and periods of lucidity. I can still do many things. I want to...to...

**HERSELF.** Participate?

**ALICE.** ...Participate in the world. I want to invite you to help me, and to help others like me, start a group so we can be with each other and know there are others like us. Did I talk long enough? Good. I will forget today. I will forget talking to you. But I hope that does not mean that my talk did not matter. Thank you.

*(Family and doctors clap and cheer.)*

**HERSELF.** *(With enthusiasm, to* **ALICE** *from the front row.)* You did great.

## Scene Twenty-One

*[March 2013]*

*(**THOMAS** enters the kitchen with a plate of chocolate brownies. **HERSELF** continues to paint while **ALICE** talks with **THOMAS**.)*

**THOMAS.** Hey Mom. *(Gives **ALICE** brownies.)* These are from Mattie. I think she made them so she could eat some. They're brownies.

**ALICE.** Oh! I love these!

**THOMAS.** I have some good news that I want to tell you. We had the baby tested for the gene mutation and she's fine. We know for sure.

**ALICE.** I'm so happy for you, Thomas. Your father is going to be happy too. Where is he?

**THOMAS.** He had to go into work tonight. He'll be back.

**ALICE.** Will you get tested?

**THOMAS.** I did, Mom, remember? I don't have the mutation. Lydia does.

**ALICE.** Oh, I'm so sorry.

**THOMAS.** By the time it hits our generation they'll have figured out a lot. Mom, I've been thinking. I'm going to take a couple months off work so I can take care of you for a while.

**ALICE.** Lydia takes care of me, and I have John. I'm okay.

**THOMAS.** Lydia is just visiting, Mom, in between plays. She doesn't live here. I live here, remember? I live here, Mom. I can help.

**ALICE.** Thank you, Tom. It's not necessary.

**THOMAS.** Mom, you don't understand. I want to. I miss our Monday lunches. For God's sake, we used to text all the time... I don't see you anymore. Please, Mom.

**ALICE.** I suppose you could read me plays, or poems. Lydia gave me a book of poetry.

**THOMAS.** Sure, Mom, I could come over and read. Or, we could go for walks, to the lake, like we used to, remember?

**ALICE.** *(Thinks this is a nice idea.)* Okay.

**THOMAS.** I could at least take a day off a week, maybe. I just want to hang out, you and me, a little. If you and Dad leave. I won't be able to just jump on a plane every... I mean, I could, I would, but the baby...

**ALICE.** I'm not going anywhere.

**THOMAS.** Right. No.

*(**THOMAS** starts to cry.)*

**HERSELF.** He seems scared for some reason.

**THOMAS.** I miss you, Mom.

**ALICE.** Tommy, have a brownie.

*(**THOMAS** eats a brownie.)*

**THOMAS.** I'll come over Friday afternoons. I'll put it in your phone for you. But I want you to call me anytime if you need something. Anything. Anytime.

**ALICE.** Okay.

*(**ALICE** exits. **THOMAS** calls after her.)*

**THOMAS.** Mom, maybe we should take all the numbers out of your phone except the most important ones.

*(**THOMAS** sits at the table, staring at the brownies.)*

## Scene Twenty-Two

*[April 2013]*

*(***ALICE*** is slowly folding clothes.* ***LYDIA*** *joins her.* ***HERSELF*** *continues to paint.)*

**LYDIA.** Mom, I got into NYU and University of Maryland!

**ALICE.** Oh, that's so exciting. I remember getting into school. I used to go to Harvard. I was a professor, you know. What school did you say you were going to?

**LYDIA.** I didn't. I'm not sure yet. Dad wants me to go to University of Maryland?

**HERSELF.** I think she wants to go to NYU.

**ALICE.** Do *you* want to go to University of Maryland?

**LYDIA.** I don't know.

**ALICE.** How old are you?

**LYDIA.** Twenty-four.

**ALICE.** I loved being twenty-four. You have your whole life in front of you. You married?

*(***LYDIA*** stops folding and looks at* ***ALICE****.)*

**LYDIA.** No. I'm not married.

**ALICE.** Kids?

**LYDIA.** No.

**ALICE.** Then you should do exactly what you want.

**LYDIA.** But what if Dad decides to take the job? I would be closer to you.

**ALICE.** You can't make this kind of decision based on what other people might or might not do. You're a grown woman. You don't have to do what your father wants.

**LYDIA.** Okay. *(Pause.)* You've come a long way, Mom.

**ALICE.** What's the name of the school you want to go to?

**LYDIA.** NYU.

**ALICE.** Really? And what are you going to study?

**LYDIA.** Acting.

**ALICE.** That's wonderful! You act in plays?

**LYDIA.** I will.

**ALICE.** Shakespeare?

**LYDIA.** Yes.

**ALICE.** I love Shakespeare. Especially the tragedies.

**LYDIA.** Me too!

(**LYDIA** *hugs* **ALICE**.)

**HERSELF.** The pretty young woman smells fresh and clean, like soap. We're happy. We feel happy.

(**LYDIA** *laughs, then* **ALICE** *and* **HERSELF** *start laughing.* **THOMAS** *enters, followed by* **JOHN**.)

**THOMAS.** *(To* **LYDIA**.*)* Dad's taking the job. And taking Mom with him.

**JOHN.** Hold on, Tom. Calm down.

**LYDIA.** Mom said you were taking sabbatical. You can start next year.

**JOHN.** She keeps saying that. She doesn't understand. It was difficult enough negotiating out to the end of summer. I need to be there in September.

**LYDIA.** Mom can stay here.

**JOHN.** No. No.

**THOMAS.** If you take her with you she'll be alone.

**JOHN.** No.

**LYDIA.** You'll be in your lab. You'll have to be.

**JOHN.** I'll have a home health aide come in every day –

**LYDIA.** A stranger. She has routines here, things that are familiar. A stranger can't love her like we can.

**JOHN.** Like *who* can? Who would take care of her here? *(To* **LYDIA** *and* **THOMAS**.*)* You? You have school. And you have work and a new baby. You're about to be busier than you've ever been, and your mother would be the last person to ask you to stop your lives. She'd never want to be a burden.

**LYDIA.** She's not a burden!

**JOHN.** Of course she's not a burden, but think about it, we'd need to have someone here every day even if I didn't take the job. Even if I took sabbatical, I couldn't take care of her alone!

**ALICE.** What's going on?

**HERSELF.** They are very serious.

**THOMAS.** So, we'll bring someone in. And I'll take a leave from work. I could get two months at least, and –

**JOHN.** Two months?!

**LYDIA.** I'll postpone school a year. No big deal. I can wait one more year.

**JOHN.** You need to work right now, and you need to go to school. You made your choices. I have to make mine.

**LYDIA.** Why doesn't Mom get a say in this? She doesn't want to leave.

**JOHN.** You don't know what she wants!

**LYDIA.** Go ahead, ask her. Just because she can't remember things doesn't mean she doesn't know what she wants. At three in the morning she wanted scrambled eggs and toast, and she didn't want cereal or bacon. And she definitely didn't want to go back to bed!

**HERSELF.** Oh, they're talking about me.

**JOHN.** She can have scrambled eggs anywhere. I *know* this is what she would want. *(Calm all of a sudden.)* Look. Come September, she won't even know who I am, who any of us are, or where she is. Being in D.C. won't matter to her.

**THOMAS.** You can't know that.

**JOHN.** You don't understand. Look. *(Near tears.)* No one loves your mother more than I do. Not you. Not anyone. Alice wouldn't want me to give up my work, who I am. If she were still herself –

**LYDIA.** She is still herself.

**JOHN.** She wouldn't even want –

**THOMAS.** What?

**JOHN.** Nothing. Look –

**LYDIA.** No, what?!

**JOHN.** No! I've thought about this. I'm trying to make a rational decision. This doesn't have to be emotional.

**LYDIA.** What's wrong with making an emotional decision? Why is a logical one best?

**JOHN.** *(Correcting her.)* Rational.

**LYDIA.** Rational! Why is *your* rational decision best?!

**JOHN.** If I don't take this job, and she's gone in September, or October, or November, or next year, I'll have nothing. Do you understand? Nothing. No job and no Alice. Nothing.

(**JOHN** *starts to cry.)*

I haven't made a decision yet, but I'm not letting you bully me into one. I'm taking Alice to the cottage. I'll let you know what I decide when we get back.

**HERSELF.** They're sad and angry. And scared. I'm not scared.

**ALICE.** I'm hungry...

## Scene Twenty-Three

*[April 2013]*

*(**HERSELF** is painting. **ALICE** sits on a chair at the beach, wrapped in a blanket. **JOHN** sits next to them. He has a briefcase and a pile of books next to him. He's reading. We hear seagulls.)*

**HERSELF.** The well-being of a neuron depends on its ability to communicate with other neurons. Studies have shown that electrical and chemical stimulation from both a neuron's inputs and its targets support vital cellular processes. Neurons unable to connect effectively with other neurons atrophy. Useless, an abandoned neuron will die.

**ALICE.** What time is it?

**HERSELF.** The man sitting in the chair will tell you.

**ALICE.** *(To* **JOHN.***)* Excuse me. What time is it?

**JOHN.** Almost 5:30.

**ALICE.** I think it's time for me to go home.

**JOHN.** You are home. This is your vacation home. Your cottage on Cape Cod. We're on vacation. You like it here.

**HERSELF.** The man, the beach, the chair don't look familiar. The sounds don't sound familiar either. I hear birds, the kind that live by the sea, the sound of the man breathing, and the ticking of the clock on his arm.

**ALICE.** I think I've been here long enough. I'd like to go home now.

**JOHN.** You are home. This is your cottage.

**ALICE.** Oh, my cottage. What are we doing here?

**JOHN.** We are relaxing. This is where you come to relax and unwind.

**ALICE.** Oh.

*(Pause.)*

*(To* **HERSELF.***)* Maybe someone will come and take me home.

(**ALICE** *picks up a book and opens it.)*

**HERSELF.** In the book there are diagrams, letters connected to other letters...

**ALICE.** I think I've read this book before.

**JOHN.** You wrote it. You and I wrote it together.

**ALICE.** *From Molecules to Mind*...by John Howland, Ph.D. ...and Alice Howland, Ph.D. *(She looks up, realizing.)* You're John.

**JOHN.** I wrote this book with you.

**HERSELF & ALICE.** I remember.

**ALICE.** I remember you. I remember I used to be smart. Very smart.

**JOHN.** Yes, you were. You were the smartest person I've ever known.

**ALICE.** I miss myself. My used to be self.

**JOHN.** I miss your used to be self too, Ali, so much.

**ALICE.** I never planned it to get like this.

**JOHN.** I know. *(Pause.)* Ali, do you still want to be here?

**ALICE.** Yes. I wanted to go home, but right now I like it here.

(**HERSELF** *gives* **ALICE** *a painting of a butterfly.* **ALICE** *places it on the sand in front of herself.)*

**HERSELF.** It's very simple, really.

**ALICE.** I like sitting here with you, a nice, handsome, sad man. *(Long pause.)* Do I need to leave now?

**JOHN.** No, take your time.

**The End**

CPSIA information can be obtained
at www.ICGtesting.com
Printed in the USA
BVHW040855130719
553084BV00007BA/203/P